Teen Activism
LIBRARY

STAND UP
for Racial Justice

Leanne Currie-McGhee

ReferencePoint
Press

San Diego, CA

For more information, contact:
ReferencePoint Press, Inc.
PO Box 27779
San Diego, CA 92198
www.ReferencePointPress.com

LIBRARY OF CONGRESS CATALOGING-IN-PUBLICATION DATA

Names: Currie-McGhee, L. K. (Leanne K.), author.
Title: Stand up for racial justice / Leanne Currie-McGhee.
Description: San Diego : ReferencePoint Press, 2021. | Series: Teen
  activism library | Includes bibliographical references and index.
Identifiers: LCCN 2021009649 (print) | LCCN 2021009650 (ebook) | ISBN
  9781678201548 (library binding) | ISBN 9781678201555 (ebook)
Subjects: LCSH: Youth--Political activity--United States--Juvenile
  literature. | Racial justice--United States--Juvenile literature. |
  Anti-racism--United States--Juvenile literature. | Social
  justice--United States--Juvenile literature.
Classification: LCC HQ799.2.P6 C87 2021 (print) | LCC HQ799.2.P6 (ebook)
  | DDC 303.3/720973--dc23
LC record available at https://lccn.loc.gov/2021009649
LC ebook record available at https://lccn.loc.gov/2021009650

CONTENTS

Time to Act

"If my mom says yes I'm leading a Nashville protest,"[1] Zee Thomas posted on Twitter at age fifteen. Thomas, a young Black woman, was inspired to do so after reacting to the death of George Floyd on May 25, 2020. Floyd, an African American man, died at the hands of a police officer during his arrest in Minneapolis, Minnesota, for allegedly using a counterfeit bill. During Floyd's arrest, police officer Derek Chauvin, who is White, knelt on Floyd's neck for several minutes. Floyd was handcuffed at the time and lying on the ground. Floyd repeatedly said, in noticeable distress, that he could not breathe. While bystanders pleaded with the officer to stop, he continued to keep his knee on Floyd's neck. After a few minutes, Floyd lay motionless. When the other officers, who had not attempted to assist Floyd until this point, checked on him, they found that he no longer had a pulse. Chauvin still would not release his knee. In fact, he kept his knee on Floyd's neck for eight minutes and forty-six seconds, according to videos of the incident. After an ambulance came, Floyd was taken to the emergency room, where he was pronounced dead. This event, which was captured on video and shared on social media, led to months-long massive protests against police brutality and racism against African Americans.

Thomas had never been to a protest before, much less led one, but after seeing what happened to Floyd, she was spurred to action. With the help of five other teenagers, Thomas organized a protest, and over ten thousand people participated. "We didn't have a podium or anything, we were standing on water coolers to speak," Thomas says. "I'm an introvert, and when I got up there

I was like, 'Oh my God, what am I doing?' But I kept going."[2] For Thomas, the protest was a way to express her own outrage about racial injustice and get others educated and interested in fighting for justice.

A Movement

Thomas was in good company. After Floyd's death, teens across the United States were motivated to become activists for the cause of racial justice. Nineteen-year-old Brianna Chandler had been involved in Black Lives Matter, an organization fighting for racial justice, since her early teens. Floyd's death increased her desire to act. She focused on educating people through social media. With the COVID-19 pandemic, many people were not going out and about, so she realized she could reach people on social media. "I posted, and then I kept thinking and writing and posting and it grew from there," Chandler explains. "What I call 'consciousness raising,' because I think that educating people is essential to movement building. There are a lot of different parts of a movement."[3] Chandler uses social media both to educate people on the issues and to organize events such as teach-ins for local high school and college students to learn about racial justice.

Like Chandler, eighteen-year-old Shayla Turner became an organizer to combat racial injustice. She worked toward a specific goal of removing police from Chicago high schools. Turner and others in her community feel that police presence in schools actually makes it more unsafe for Black students and other minority students, because statistics show they are disproportionately arrested

and disciplined compared to White students. Turner believes that funding for school counselors and psychologists and counseling programs would be an effective alternative to funding police in schools. In 2020 Turner worked toward this goal, even during her own high school graduation week. She did so by organizing email chains and a petition drive. She sent the emails and petitions to the head of Chicago Public Schools, requesting funding for these services in place of police in the schools.

Rising Teen Interest

Turner, Chandler, and Thomas are just three of the many teen activists for racial justice. According to a 2020 poll released by the Advancement Project National Office, a civil rights organization, 78 percent of young American voters of color took activist actions in 2020. These actions included signing a petition, posting or sharing information about racial issues on social media, and participating in a protest.

Young people are taking activist stances on issues that matter to them because they believe they can make a difference. A 2020 youth survey by CIRCLE/Tisch College found that 83 percent of young people believe they have the power to change the country. Chandler affirms that this is one reason why she and many young people she knows have become involved in racial justice activism.

They also see how racism affects their lives and the lives of other people. This provides powerful motivation to stay involved even when doing so leads to exhaustion. "Young people bring radical hope to this movement. While that should be appreciated, it shouldn't be romanticized," Chandler explains. "It is a burden to be deeply aware of the injustices in this country while actively working to dismantle them. I've seen so many young organizers push themselves beyond burnout because dismantling racism is literally a life or death matter."[4]

> **"Young people bring radical hope to this movement."[4]**
>
> —Brianna Chandler, youth activist

CHAPTER ONE

The Issue Is Racial Justice

Keyon Harrold Jr., age fourteen, and his father, Keyon Harrold, a Grammy Award–winning jazz musician, did not expect to be verbally and physically assaulted on December 26, 2020, while standing in a New York City hotel lobby. Father and son had stayed at the hotel and were in the lobby before going to breakfast. Suddenly, a young woman named Miya Ponsetto started screaming at Keyon, accusing the teen of stealing her phone when she saw he was holding a phone. As Kenyon attempted to walk away, Ponsetto rushed up to him, tackled him, and demanded that he return her phone. The hotel manager got involved, asking Keyon to show his phone. Upset at essentially being accused of stealing with no basis for such an accusation, Keyon and his father started to walk away. Ponsetto continued to scream at them. The entire scene was captured on his father's cell phone video and posted to social media. Later, Ponsetto's phone was found by an Uber driver; Ponsetto had apparently left her phone in his car. She was eventually arrested for assaulting Keyon.

Many believe Ponsetto's attack on Keyon was based on racism and that she accused him of stealing because he is Black. New York City mayor Bill de Blasio supported Keyon and his father and said that Ponsetto acted on "racism, plain and simple."[5] Many similar incidents have been captured on cell phone videos. Regardless of age, Black Americans are often falsely accused of crimes by others. These are examples of racial injustice, when people are treated differently and unfairly because of their race. Being falsely accused or even arrested because of one's race is just one type of racial injustice. Multitudes of racial injustice incidents occur daily throughout the United States, affecting people of color during their dealings with law enforcement, education, housing, and more.

Problem from the Past

Racial injustice in the United States has its roots in the founding of the country. Settlers arriving from Europe felt it was their right to take over indigenous lands. Many people had no problem doing whatever was necessary to achieve that goal. Slavery is also a legacy of America's founding. African men, women, and children were ripped from their native lands and shipped to the Americas to work as slaves on farms, in fields, and in people's homes. They were property to be bought and sold. They had no rights. They were viewed as subhuman and treated that way by their White owners and by others.

Keyon Harrold Sr. (center), a Grammy Award–winning jazz musician, holds a press conference after his son was attacked by a woman who wrongly accused him of stealing her phone. Many believe the assault on the men was racially biased.

These beginnings informed the way many White Americans viewed people of color, whether Africans or Native Americans. It was not until after the Civil War and after slavery had been made unconstitutional that male African Americans and Native Americans were granted citizenship by the Fourteenth Amendment and the right to vote by the Fifteenth Amendment. Despite this progress, racism did not end. Many White Americans continued to see people of color as lesser beings. Jim Crow laws diminished the rights of people of color in voting, jobs, and education. Segregated schools and neighborhoods further promoted and reinforced unequal treatment of Black Americans.

Activists for racial justice—among them Martin Luther King Jr., John Lewis, and Rosa Parks—have fought against such discrimination and have won many victories. However, even with greater rights legally secured, centuries of being viewed and treated as second-class citizens has led to systemic racism. This is racism that is entrenched in society due to the treatment and views of the past.

Law Enforcement

Systemic racism in law enforcement has gained high-profile visibility in the past few years. The killing of George Floyd set off months of protests and action against racism in law enforcement, but it is just one of many incidents involving police killings of unarmed Black Americans. Many of the names are by now familiar. In 2014 twelve-year-old Tamir Rice was shot and killed by police in Cleveland, Ohio. He had been holding a toy gun. In North Charleston, South Carolina, in 2015 Walter Scott was stopped by police for a minor traffic violation. He attempted to flee on foot. Police shot him in the back, killing him. In 2018 an off-duty Dallas, Texas, police officer mistakenly entered the apartment of Botham Jean, a twenty-six-year-old accountant. The officer thought she had entered her own apartment and that Jean was an intruder. She shot and killed him. And in March 2020 in Louisville, Kentucky, Breonna Taylor was shot and killed by police who burst into her apartment looking for a suspect who no longer lived there.

Protesters hold a sign picturing Breonna Taylor at a Black Lives Matter march in Los Angeles. In March 2020, Taylor was shot and killed by White police officers who burst into her apartment looking for a suspect who no longer lived there. Critics believe the officers used excessive force.

The common denominator in all of these killings is that the victims were Black. Critics believe the officers would have acted differently if the individuals had been White. For instance, many believe police would not have forced entry into Taylor's apartment if she had been White. "I do not believe Taylor's case is unique. Police break into black and brown people's residences, unannounced, all around the country," writes Elie Mystal, criminal justice writer for the *Nation*. "I believe that some of those residents attempt to defend themselves from what they think is a home invasion. Police then use that attempted defense as justification for gunning them down."[6]

> "Police break into black and brown people's residences, unannounced, all around the country."[6]
>
> —Elie Mystal, correspondent on racial justice

Advocates for racial justice believe that Taylor's shooting displays the devastating effects of injustice against Black people by

Not only are those of color more at risk of being racially profiled and arrested, but once they are convicted of a crime, racial disparities continue. The US Sentencing Commission found that Black men who are convicted of the same crimes as White men receive 20 percent longer sentences in federal prison. The commission reviewed demographic prison data from 2012 to 2016. The differences in prison sentences were found even after the researchers controlled for other sentencing factors such as age, education, weapon possession, and past criminal history.

A major reason for the differences in sentencing, according to the report, is that sentencing is often at the judge's discretion. The report concluded that judges are less likely to decrease sentences for Black offenders than White offenders when they have the choice to do so. In cases where judges do reduce Black offenders' sentences, overall, they do so in smaller amounts than for White offenders. As a result, Black criminals with similar histories stay in jail longer for the same crimes compared to White criminals.

law enforcement. According to the *Washington Post*, from 2015 to 2020, Black Americans were shot by police officers at a much higher rate than White Americans. While Black Americans make up less than 13 percent of the population, 24 percent of those shot by police were Black. Why is this so?

Racial Profiling

Racial profiling—which could be described as a symptom of systemic racism in law enforcement—may be one reason. Racial profiling, according to the American Civil Liberties Union (ACLU), "refers to the discriminatory practice by law enforcement officials of targeting individuals for suspicion of crime based on the individual's race, ethnicity, religion or national origin."[7] When police decide to pull a driver over for a minor infraction because of his or her race, that is racial profiling. A 2020 study published in the journal *Nature Human Behaviour* reinforces the view that this is happening. The nationwide study found that of nearly 100 million traffic stops from 2011 to 2018, on average Black drivers were pulled over 20 percent more often than White drivers.

Tae-Ahn Lea, age eighteen, has experienced this firsthand. Lea, who is Black, was driving his mother's car in Louisville, Kentucky, when he was pulled over for a minor traffic infraction—making a wide turn. Lea, homecoming king and the recipient of many college scholarships, was pulled out of the car, frisked, and handcuffed. Officers even had the car searched by a drug-sniffing dog. No drugs were found, and the traffic violation was dismissed. Critics say this is one of many examples of over-policing and targeting people of color.

Race and Education

Racial injustice exists in other areas of modern life. One of these is education. Racial segregation in public education was once sanctioned by US law. Black students were barred from attending public schools with White students under the doctrine that came to be known as separate but equal. The legal theory underpinning this doctrine was that students could be segregated as long as the schools were of equal quality. In reality, schools for Black youth and White youth were anything but equal. In a landmark 1954 case, the Supreme Court put an end to this doctrine. In the case of *Brown v. Board of Education*, the court ruled unanimously that racial segregation of children in public schools was unconstitutional. But, activists contend, the legacy of segregated schools continues for many Black Americans.

Although the law no longer sanctions segregation, many schools remain segregated by virtue of where people live. Many US cities have neighborhoods that are mostly Black, White, Latino, or Asian. Because students usually attend public schools in their own neighborhoods, the schools tend to have a high number of one group or another. The nonprofit organization EdBuild reported in 2019 that more than half of students attend schools with a high concentration of either White or non-White students. This is a problem because predominantly White school districts receive billions of dollars more per year than predominantly non-White school districts, according to

A defining characteristic of the racial justice activism that started in 2020 and has been ongoing since is how diverse the participation is. Dana Fisher, a professor of sociology at the University of Maryland, has collected data from four different 2020 protests in Los Angeles, New York City, and Washington, DC. She found that 54 percent of those protesting were White. Fisher writes that these protests are more diverse than the March for Racial Justice of 2017, Black Lives Matter protests in previous years, and protests during the civil rights movement. Sociologist Doug McAdam writes, "We have never seen protests like these before, in turnout, perseverance, and the ethnic and racial diversity of those participating."

What does this mean for the movement? To Fisher and others, it signifies increased likelihood for racial justice to be obtained, since it means that more people, of all races, believe in the need for equity and are calling for changes. She contends that when there is solidarity between different groups, there is a greater chance at instituting change.

Quoted in Dana Fisher, "The Diversity of the Recent Black Lives Matter Protests Is a Good Sign for Racial Equity," *How We Rise* (blog), Brookings Institution, July 8, 2020. www.brookings.edu.

EdBuild. The nonprofit organization Education Trust also found that districts serving the most students of color receive roughly $1,800 less per student than those serving the fewest students of color. This is tied to the fact that a large part of school funding comes from local property taxes, and mainly non-White neighborhoods are generally areas with lower property values. According to Ivy Morgan of Education Trust, "When local property taxes form the foundation of school funding systems, it compounds the impact of injustices inflicted on communities of color outside the school by systematically underfunding their children inside of school."[8]

Less funding means lower teacher salaries and smaller budgets for programs and technology, leading to a lower quality of education in schools primarily attended by students of color. According to the US Department of Education, a quarter of high schools with the highest percentage of Black and Latino students do not offer Algebra II, and one-third of these schools do not offer chemistry. The 2015–2016 Civil Rights Data Collection survey found that only 38 percent of mainly minority schools offered calculus, compared to 50 percent of all high schools. And just over half of predominantly minority schools offered physics, compared to 60 percent of high schools overall. Lack of these courses leads to fewer opportunities for getting into colleges and limits options of STEM (science, technology, engineering, and mathematics) careers.

Activists cite other education-related issues as examples of racial injustice. One of these involves how schools discipline students. A US Department of Education study of K–12 public schools found that Black students are almost four times as likely to be suspended and almost twice as likely to be expelled as White students. Missing classes and school leads to lower grades and falling behind academically, both of which lessen opportunities for higher education and increase the likelihood of dropping out.

Housing

Activists point to housing as another area where people are affected by racial injustice. It is harder for Black Americans to obtain their own homes due to greater difficulty obtaining home loans. In the first quarter of 2020, only 44 percent of Black families owned homes, compared to 73.7 percent of White families, according to the US Census Bureau.

"The Black community is unfairly being charged higher interest rates and refinance costs—a practice that is deeply rooted in systematic racism."[9]

—Samuel Deane, financial planner

One reason is that obtaining a home loan with average interest rates is more difficult for people of color, even if they have similar income levels and credit history. "Race and ethnicity should not be a factor in determining lending decisions. Yet, even with similar creditworthiness, whether face to face or online, the Black community is unfairly being charged higher interest rates and refinance costs—a practice that is deeply rooted in systematic racism,"[9] says financial planner Samuel Deane.

The difficulty of obtaining loans dates back to the 1930s, when banks routinely (and legally) prevented Black people from obtaining loans for buying a home. Maps of neighborhoods with predominantly Black residents were outlined in red (called redlining) to indicate that banks should not give home loans to people living in these neighborhoods. Although redlining is no longer legal, a 2020 Zillow analysis of data from the Home Mortgage Disclosure Act shows that lenders deny loans for Black people at a rate 80 percent higher than that of White applicants.

A reason for denying loans to Black people today is that, in general, they do not have the same level of credit history as others. Credit history is the biggest factor in determining credit scores—and credit scores determine whether a person obtains a loan. Credit history is currently determined mainly by a person's payment history of paying credit cards on time. One reason this harms Americans of color is that it is more difficult for them to obtain credit cards and build a credit history. According to a 2019 report by the Federal Reserve, 5 percent of Whites were unable to access a credit card compared to 32 percent of African Americans and 28 percent of Latinos. Without a credit history, a person cannot obtain a good credit score.

Senator Tim Scott of South Carolina believes the method for determining credit scores is outdated and discriminatory. The current method "does not take into account consumer data on rent, utility, and cellphone bill payments," wrote Scott when, in 2019, he introduced a bill that would change credit standards for obtaining home loans. "This exclusion disproportionately hurts African-Americans, Latinos, and young people who are otherwise creditworthy."[10] Scott believes that a credit score should also be determined by a person's history of paying monthly costs such as rent, utilities such as electricity, and cell phone bills on time. He believes that these are positive indicators that a person is capable of paying back a loan. If ability to pay monthly costs is included, Scott feels that, on average, a person of color would obtain a higher credit score.

Nupol Kiazolu, president of Black Lives Matter of Greater New York, holds a rally in New York City on August 11, 2019, before embarking on a march.

Righting the Wrongs

Racial justice is about fixing injustices such as those in housing, education, and law enforcement. Racial justice activists have pushed for and achieved progress over the years. In the 1960s US citizens saw great strides in the fight for civil rights. Congress passed the 1964 Civil Rights Act, which required the desegregation of schools; protected all people's right to vote; outlawed all types of discrimination based on a person's race, color, religion, sex, or national origin; and required equal access to public places and employment. Since then, more achievements such as greater diversity at colleges, in workplaces, and in all institutions have occurred, and racial barriers have increasingly been broken. Still, the effects of racism continue, which is why the work toward racial justice continues.

In 2020 a great surge of work toward racial justice occurred after the George Floyd killing. His death sparked nationwide protests and activism meant to force people to see that racism still exists in the United States and work to fix it. Progress from these efforts has occurred since then. Law enforcement agencies throughout the country are changing their policies. For one, the Minneapolis City Council voted to ban police chokeholds and to require officers to get involved if they see another officer using unauthorized force on a person. As another example, in 2020 Iowa governor Kim Reynolds signed a police reform bill into law that prohibits the use of chokeholds in arrests unless the person cannot be captured in any other way, requires antibias and de-escalation training, and prevents hiring an officer who was previously fired for misconduct. Other changes like this were made in cities throughout the United States.

As progress is made, there is now perhaps even stronger determination to finally bring about change in law enforcement and other areas—to finally transform racial injustice into racial justice. Teens are playing a major role in this transformation through all types of activism, from protests to petition drives. Alana Mitchell, a Black student from Dr. Martin Luther King, Jr. Early College, a middle and high school in Denver, Colorado, and friends worked together to convince their school board to include more African American studies in the district's curriculum. As of 2020, they had ensured that an African American studies course would be included at their own school, with plans to expand to more. Mitchell is one of the teens who has stepped up to find ways toward racial justice. Nupol Kiazolu, the president of Black Lives Matter of Greater New York and currently a college student at Hampton University, speaks of the importance of being involved in the work toward racial justice: "Because at the end of the day, we are not only the future of this country, but we're the present. And if we don't have it, we don't stand up, then who will?"[11]

CHAPTER TWO

The Activists

The twentieth century saw the rise of civil rights organizations such as the National Association for the Advancement of Colored People (NAACP) and civil rights leaders such as Martin Luther King Jr. Through speeches, boycotts, sit-ins, marches, lawsuits, and lobbying, the civil rights activists of an earlier era made impressive gains in the areas of education, voting rights, outlawing racial segregation, and more. And yet racial inequality persists in the United States. The twenty-first century has seen the rise of a new generation of activists who are focused once again on issues of racial justice.

Black Lives Matter

Among the most influential of the newer racial justice activist organizations is Black Lives Matter (BLM). It has made an impact nationally and internationally with the help of teens and young adults who have taken a stance and been at the center of BLM organizing efforts. BLM was founded in 2013 by Alicia Garza, Opal Tometi, and Patrisse Cullors after the killing of seventeen-year-old Trayvon Martin. Martin, who was African American, had been walking in a gated Florida neighborhood. He and his father were there to visit the father's fiancée. When George Zimmerman, a neighborhood watch coordinator, saw Martin, he thought Martin looked suspicious and called police. Police told Zimmerman to take no action and to wait for their arrival. Zimmerman

The mid-twentieth century saw the rise of civil rights leaders such as Martin Luther King Jr. (pictured). The twenty-first century has seen the rise of a new generation of activists who are focused once again on issues of racial justice.

ignored this advice, instead confronting Martin and chasing after him when the teen walked away. This led to a physical altercation that resulted in Zimmerman shooting Martin, who was unarmed. Martin died from the gunshot wound. Zimmerman was tried and acquitted on a charge of second-degree murder.

The verdict shocked people nationwide. Martin, they believed, was targeted due to his race, and Zimmerman, they contended, would not have been acquitted if Martin were White. Frustrated and outraged, Garza, Tometi, and Cullors began posting their views on social media and using the hashtag #blacklivesmatter. After this, they increased their actions by informally bringing people together to participate in protests against violent acts committed against Black Americans—especially police killings of unarmed Black men and women. By 2016, BLM had become a national network of over thirty groups focused on changing law enforcement practices that reinforce systemic racism. Today BLM is a global organization with active groups in the United States, United Kingdom, and Canada.

BLM's prominence as an activist organization on racial justice issues grew in 2020 after the death of George Floyd. Despite the limitations on life during the COVID-19 pandemic, an estimated 15 million to 26 million people participated in BLM protests in the United States in 2020. Protesters focused their attention on police killings of unarmed African Americans and demanded changes in policing tactics, policies, and practices. BLM activists also called for broader changes that would give priority to funding services that help, as opposed to punishing, people of color. Through protests, email campaigns, petition drives, and other activities, BLM activists have made their mark. Their work has been central to efforts aimed at bringing about change. In 2020, for instance, New York City reduced its police budget by $1 billion, reallocating that money to mental health, homelessness, and education. Similarly, Los Angeles reduced its proposed police budget by $150 million and San Francisco by $120 million, putting that money toward services within Black communities instead. These changes support calls by BLM to prioritize preventive services in communities of color over punitive actions by police.

Teens Take Action Through BLM

Teens had a major impact on BLM's 2020 successes, often organizing their own protests and activities to call for social justice. "When I saw the video of George Floyd, I didn't feel the way I should've felt," says Anya Dillard, age seventeen. "It felt more like, 'Oh my gosh, again?' The shock of it becoming so normal in my mind threw me into an emotional whirlwind. I had to shut everything off and reevaluate my purpose."[12] Dillard and a group of West Orange, New Jersey, students organized a BLM protest to call for changes in policing. They also gathered more than six thousand signatures on a petition for police reform in their city. Their goals include bans on chokeholds, tear gas, and racial profiling.

Like Dillard, Thandiwe Abdullah, age sixteen, is an organizer for the BLM movement. She is a cofounder of BLM Youth Vanguard in the Los Angeles Unified School District. BLM Youth Vanguard is focused on justice for Black children, particularly those in school. Abdullah helped develop the Black Lives Matter in Schools program, which is a curriculum to educate students about and promote racial justice discussions and zero tolerance for racism at schools. The National Education Association, which represents teachers and other school personnel, has promoted the use of this program in schools across the country. Another effort of Abdullah while working with BLM Youth Vanguard was to stop random student searches for drugs and weapons by police in schools. These searches, according to the ACLU, often disproportionately target minorities. Efforts to end these types of searches in the district were successful. Now Abdullah and the organization are focused on removing police from the schools, because they believe that minorities are unfairly targeted and criminalized in school. For Abdullah, being an activist with BLM throughout middle school and now high school is a calling, despite being difficult. "Grappling with confidence in being a strong Black girl was one of the hardest things I ever had to [do]," explains Abdullah. "But I constantly reminded myself of the why. I did the work for justice, and that kept me going."[13]

"Grappling with confidence in being a strong Black girl was one of the hardest things I ever had to. But I constantly reminded myself of the why. I did the work for justice, and that kept me going."[13]

—Thandiwe Abdullah, activist

Color of Change

Another influential racial justice organization is Color of Change, the largest online racial justice organization. Established in 2005 to give African Americans a greater political voice, it organizes and

Sibling Team

Aly Conyers and her brother, Ace, were moved to action after the killing of George Floyd. The two teens from South Carolina had previously taken part in BLM protests. This time they decided to form their own group. They call it Faces of the Future. "My brother and I were really moved to have our own protest," Aly says. "We thought we'd get a lot of young people out in a very organized way for our voices to be heard. So we created a protest at Howard University, and it actually turned out really big. Since then we've had two others."

Faces of the Future also focused on getting people registered to vote in 2020. "Our priorities are making sure people understand what we're fighting for. We're making sure people know their rights, and also going out to vote," Aly stated, although she was too young to vote in the 2020 election. "I feel like we can always change the system from within, and that means electing the right person to reflect that." The Conyers work as a team to bring about change in their community.

Quoted in Precious Fondren, "Young Black Activists Are Leading the Movement for Black Lives," *Teen Vogue*, July 9, 2020. www.teenvogue.com.

leads online actions against police brutality, racial stereotypes in television and movies, and other forms of racial injustice. The group uses a variety of online tools to organize boycotts and circulate petitions and fund-raising letters, among other actions. Through its extensive online network of more than 7 million members, Color of Change has helped elect candidates who are sensitive to racial justice concerns and persuaded credit card companies to stop processing donations to White supremacist groups.

Color of Change has gained public attention through several campaigns, including one involving Facebook. In 2020 the organization organized an advertiser boycott of the social media giant in order to get the company to take a more aggressive stance against hate speech posted on its site. Color of Change reached out to several companies on its own. In June 2020 it also joined with other groups who together placed an advertisement in the *Los Angeles Times* requesting that companies stop buying ads on Facebook until Facebook changed its hate speech policies. Hundreds of companies responded by halting their advertising. Eventually,

Facebook agreed to take greater steps to fight against hate speech on its site. Color of Change executive director Rashad Robinson says more action is needed, but at least it is a start. "While [the campaign] hasn't led to as many changes as I would like, my little civil rights organization is taking on the biggest communications platform the world has ever known. And has forced a scenario in which Mark [Zuckerberg] and Sheryl [Sandberg] have to deal with our attacks, which are rooted in their failures, and also have to still work with us,"[14] Robinson explains.

Another victory for Color of Change occurred in 2020, when the television show *COPS* was canceled. Color of Change led the years-long effort to cancel the show, which it says normalized over-policing and use of excessive force and reinforced racial profiling. The organization's campaign centered on an online petition drive. The signed petitions were sent to advertisers and the Fox network, which hosted the show. Robinson says, "Research shows that with such a narrow range of Black characters and personalities in primetime, the negative perceptions and distorted images presented by shows like *COPS*, create an atmosphere of suspicion and desensitizes and conditions audiences to view police misconduct and harsher punishments as acceptable."[15]

Color of Change has attracted involvement from college athletes with its endorsement of the College Athletes Bill of Rights. Its members have been advocating for federal legislation guaranteeing fair pay for student athletes in colleges across the country. Colleges earn big money from sports like football and basketball. Critics believe the athletes, many of whom are Black, should share in that bounty. In 2020 Senator Cory Booker of New Jersey introduced such legislation, with major support from Color of Change.

The organization's involvement in this issue has attracted student athletes (and nonathletes). Tori Carroll, a Black sophomore track and field athlete at DePaul University, supports Color of Change in this and other causes. She has signed its petitions as a way to fight for justice and revise policies throughout the country.

Because much of Color of Change's advocacy is online, through petitions and letters, it is easy for a young adult or teenager to become involved.

The NAACP

The NAACP has been fighting for racial justice for over a century. It has more than five hundred thousand members worldwide and a strong youth contingent. The group's primary goal is to eradicate race-based discrimination by making sure that all Americans have equal rights and equal opportunities in education, housing, health, voting, the workplace, the criminal justice system, and more.

Throughout its history, the NAACP has devoted its considerable resources to challenging discriminatory laws and policies. It has done this through lawsuits, protests, boycotts, lobbying, and other actions. The organization has had many successes in the courts, including the Supreme Court ruling in the 1954 *Brown v. Board of Education* case. The NAACP has also been instrumental in lobbying for passage of landmark legislation, including the Civil Rights Act of 1964 and the Voting Rights Act of 1965.

High school students Erika Alvarez, Foyin Dosunmu, and Jeffrey Jin started Katy4Justice in Katy, Texas, as a way to promote social justice and allow young people to have a voice in the world. After organizing a protest against racial injustice in law enforcement, in the summer of 2020 they created a Facebook page to educate others about racism, discuss what can be done, and provide a place for students to share their own experiences.

Many students have submitted stories of their own personal experiences with racism. For example, in February 2021 an Asian American student wrote that she and other students of Asian ancestry were being harassed because of their background. Some were asked if they had "kung fu flu," due to COVID-19 originating in China. And she had been asked if she had "bat soup" in her backpack, due to speculation that the virus may have crossed over to humans from bats.

More recently, the NAACP challenged the Trump administration policy on Deferred Action for Childhood Arrivals, better known as DACA. DACA is a program that allows undocumented immigrants who were brought to the United States as children to officially remain in the country without fear of deportation if they register and are working and/or attending school. In 2017 the Trump administration rescinded DACA, putting the program's approximately 650,000 young adults in danger of deportation. The NAACP filed a lawsuit to block this action, and in 2020 the Supreme Court ruled against the Trump administration in NAACP's favor. Derrick Johnson, president and CEO of the NAACP, stated:

Today's Supreme Court ruling in our favor is an incredible victory for justice, in the spirit of the NAACP's groundbreaking Supreme Court victory in *Brown v Board of Education*. We know the value of affirmative litigation to ensure that the nation lives up to its ideals. This ruling exemplifies the ways in which ensuring the Civil Rights for our community pushes the needle on social justice for the benefit of all.[16]

The NAACP has also been actively involved in increasing voting rights and voter turnout among Blacks and other minorities. For instance, the group had an active role in bringing out Black voters in key states during the November 2020 election. The NAACP's Black Voices Change Lives campaign relied on thousands of volunteers making in-person visits, a mass texting and advertising campaign, and other forms of outreach. The campaign connected with millions of Black voters, who turned out to vote and helped elect Democrat Joe Biden as president.

NAACP Youth Activism

Youth involvement in the NAACP is significant, with over twenty-five thousand young people under age twenty-five involved in over 550 Junior Youth Councils, Youth Councils, High School Chapters, and College Chapters. The role of these groups is to develop leadership skills in youth and for them to use these skills to engage in and lead activism for social justice causes important in their communities. In 2020 many of these groups organized protests for racial justice after the killing of George Floyd, and youth leaders spoke at the protests. One such event, in June 2020, was organized by the Michigan State Youth and College Division of the NAACP. They led a We Are Done Dying protest for reform, justice, and equality in Lansing, Michigan. More than one thousand people took part in the demonstration.

That same year, many NAACP youth groups also focused on getting Black citizens out to vote for candidates who supported racial justice. For example, youth members of the organization were key in getting out the vote for the presidential election and the Georgia special election for the Senate that followed. Volunteers tweeted, texted, called, and hosted events (while following COVID-19 precautions) to increase Black voter turnout. For example, in Waco, Texas, the NAACP organized sixty-five high school and college volunteers who handed out water, snacks, phone chargers, lawn chairs, and umbrellas on Election Day in order to encourage people to wait and vote, even in long lines.

"It makes me feel excited about the future of our country," Waco NAACP president Peaches Henry says. "I am never one of those people who thinks that young people are not engaged in the political process. They absolutely are, and I know that because when I put out the request for volunteers for Election Day, I actually got close to 100 [responses] in less than a 2-hour period."[17]

Youth-Led Organizations

While many young people have become involved in the fight for racial justice by joining established organizations, others have created their own groups. Youth activists have taken the initiative to focus on specific racial justice goals, and they have organized events and actions to work toward these goals.

After the death of George Floyd, nineteen-year-old Madison Crenshaw of Atlanta, Georgia, felt the need to do something. She wanted people to know that he died because of racial injustice and to give others a voice to talk about what happened. Crenshaw organized Buckhead for Black Lives, a youth-led organization working for racial justice in Atlanta's Buckhead neighborhood. The group's first event was a protest. Crenshaw and several friends created a digital flyer and put it on their social media accounts. Together, they had over ten thousand followers, so it reached many people. They decided on a 3.2-mile (5.1 km) protest route that took them from a parking lot of a shopping center to the Governor's Mansion on June 7, 2020. Crenshaw could not believe how many people turned out for the march. "I remember looking around and it was a sea of people. I was surprised, shocked and overwhelmed," she explains. "I really have to thank social media. I never would've thought in a million years we'd be able to get 2,000 people to attend and be in support of our march."[18]

> "I am never one of those people who thinks that young people are not engaged in the political process. They absolutely are."[17]
>
> —Peaches Henry, Waco, Texas, NAACP president

Black Lives Matter activists in Portland, Oregon, hold a sign protesting the shooting death of Quanice Hayes. Hayes's death inspired two local high school students to form the organization Raising Justice, with the goal of transforming the Portland police system.

Like Crenshaw, Taji Chesimet and Britt Masback also felt the need to act. The two Portland, Oregon, high school students were motivated by the February 2017 police shooting death of Quanice Hayes, a Black seventeen-year-old in their community. Chesimet and Masback formed Youth Educating Police, now called Raising Justice, with the goal of transforming Portland's police system. According to Masback, their goals include

> trying to reduce over policing of low-level offenses or patrolling and enforcement in certain communities. Taking out school officers is one way of divesting like has just occurred here in Portland and many other cities. We want to assess what the community wants, where they want police to step back, and then mandate police policies to do that, whether it's reducing personnel or defunding other programs.[19]

One of their major accomplishments, funded through grants they applied for and received, in 2020 was to initiate and conduct a training curriculum with the Portland Police Bureau. The organization provided youth facilitators who conducted in-person and video training to over one thousand officers on how to better deal with youth, particularly minority youth, in order to decrease use of force and improve interactions between youth and police. By the summer of 2020, the organization had developed teams in five cities working toward police reform and community engagement.

"We want to assess what the community wants, where they want police to step back, and then mandate police policies to do that, whether it's reducing personnel or defunding other programs."[19]

—Britt Masback, cofounder of Raising Justice

Whether through student-led organizations or involvement in national groups, young people play an essential role as activists for racial justice. They have grown up seeing the effects of systemic racism on people's lives, including their own, and want to have a voice for change. Whether through encouraging more positive interactions with police, getting out the vote, or protesting for changes in the legal system, their voices are being heard.

CHAPTER THREE

The Teen Activist's Tool Kit

Youth across the United States and around the world joined the fight for racial justice in 2020. Many took on leadership roles in existing organizations; some even founded their own organizations. They were inspired by the need for change and decided to take action. These young people found that the most effective ways to become involved in racial justice activism involved educating themselves, communicating their ideas to others, and organizing actions that would lead to change.

These are the steps Arlette Morales of York, Pennsylvania, followed on her journey to becoming an activist for social justice. Morales began by fighting for undocumented immigrants in the DACA program as a young teen. This fight is personal; Morales is one of the nearly six hundred fifty thousand young people who were DACA recipients as of 2020.

Then, after George Floyd's death, she expanded her activism to the BLM movement. However, she felt that she needed to know more about the racial injustices that affect all people of color. She began by educating herself. She read more about the events surrounding Floyd's death and discussed what she was reading with her friend Tzipporah Goins. The two continued to read and learn about other incidents. One of these was the 2020 death of Ahmaud Arbery, a Black man killed by a White father and son while he was jogging in a Georgia neighborhood. They also read articles that cited statistics about injustices faced by Black Americans. At this point, Morales decided to act. "I was like a volcano," Morales says. "And I wanted to explode with my voice. And I wanted to use my voice."[20]

She posted her thoughts on Facebook, using the platform to also organize a protest for justice and accountability. Within a day, more than seven hundred people had responded. Morales and Goins set about organizing the event. They worked with police and the mayor to ensure that they were following local laws and the protest could occur safely. Their protest took place on June 2, 2020, in York, Pennsylvania. Over fifteen hundred people, including many young people who later asked for tips on organizing events, turned out. Following the protest, Morales planned for more events and action to fight for racial and social justice. These included events to register people to vote and supporting Black-owned businesses in her community. She planned to continue her fight for immigrant and racial justice after graduating high school in 2021.

Learn About the Issues

Being passionate about a cause is great, but passion without knowledge is likely to be very limiting. The most effective activists take time to learn about the issues that matter to them. There are plenty of ways to do this. Books, news articles, academic studies, organization reports, documentaries, and discussion with other people (those who share similar views and those who do not) can all help activists build a knowledge base. The seeds of activism were planted for Carrie Mays when she moved from a predominantly White suburb to the more racially diverse city of Dorchester, Massachusetts. Mays, nineteen, is Black and a sophomore in college. To Mays the quality of education and opportunities in housing and careers seemed more limited for African Americans living in the city than for residents of the mostly White suburbs. "I wanted to get to the bottom of that because I felt like I was seeing the effects of racism, but I wasn't seeing the root causes,"[21] she explains. She started investigating the causes by reading news articles and opinion pieces and talking to people. She also joined Teen Empowerment, a nonprofit group that focuses on encouraging urban youth to think about issues affecting them and their communities and makes sure they have the skills to address those issues. The skills and knowledge Mays gained in this group led to her activism on challenging systemic racism. Mays now organizes events such as group discussions on race, serves as a speaker and panelist at racial justice events, and attends and helps others organize protests.

Young aspiring activists can also learn from those already involved in activism and can gain a better understanding both of the

Cell phones can be very effective tools for young activists. They can easily research an issue online and then share their thoughts and organize protests through social media.

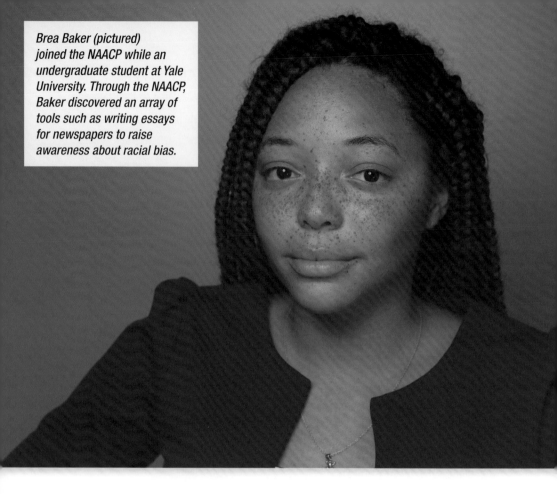

Brea Baker (pictured) joined the NAACP while an undergraduate student at Yale University. Through the NAACP, Baker discovered an array of tools such as writing essays for newspapers to raise awareness about racial bias.

issues and of ways to take action. Brea Baker joined the NAACP while an undergraduate at Yale University. By listening to the experiences of other students, Baker learned about worrisome events taking place at Yale. For instance, many colleges have stopped using the term *master* when referring to the leaders of their residential colleges because of the word's connotation from the days of slavery. Yale, however, was still using that term. Baker also heard from a group of Black college women who were turned away from a fraternity party after they were told that the party was for White women only.

Through the NAACP, Baker discovered an array of tools she could use to call attention to these types of issues. These tools included writing essays for newspapers, organizing sit-ins, and talking about and teaching others about bias. Baker became an NAACP chapter president in 2015. This allowed her not only to participate in but also to lead events and campaigns for social justice. The tools she obtained as a student have served her well in her ongoing activism for racial justice.

Communication

Communication is central to activism. If you cannot convey your ideas to others in a way that they can understand, there is little chance of getting agreement or action. The good news is that there are plenty of ways to communicate. Social media is the tool of choice for today's activists because it is the fastest way to reach a lot of people.

Ohi Oni-Eseleh is one of many activists who have found their voice on social media. After the death of George Floyd, many of his White friends expressed surprise and concern about the events and wanted to know what they could do. He saw this as an opportunity to educate. Oni-Eseleh says:

> As a Black man in this country, I didn't have the luxury of being shocked by the murder of a Black man, and so it was overwhelming to try to process my own emotions while also trying to process the individual surprise. As a way to codify my feelings and my thoughts on the topic and invert the conversation from the many-to-one to the one-to-many, I decided to take to Instagram.[22]

Since Floyd's death, Oni-Eseleh has regularly posted his personal thoughts and experiences about racial injustice in the United States and how people can support the BLM movement. He does this in hopes of getting more people to think about and become involved in racial justice activism. And his words are reaching many; by March 2021, he had over 21,000 followers.

Letter writing, while considered by many to be old-fashioned, can be another useful tool for activists. Nadia Adams and Joyce Liow both graduated in 2020 from Brighton Central School District schools in Rochester, New York. Although the district's student

Kenneth, a Black university student in Massachusetts, gets frustrated when he sees classmates posting vacation photos on Instagram. He uses his social media account to answer questions about race and the BLM movement. He would like to see more people engaging in these sorts of discussions on social media. His own experiences with racism and the unfolding events of 2020 left him feeling the need to take part in these types of discussions. He sees social media as a way to do this.

Kenneth has turned his own Instagram account into a forum for questions and answers about being Black in America and about the goals of BLM. Kenneth has been encouraged by the responses and interest he has received on his account. He explains:

> I recently had a question and answer session on my Instagram, in which I encouraged people to submit their questions to me anonymously. The over-all response to it was crazy—I thought I was going to just answer like five or six questions, but I ended up spending almost an hour answering questions on the Black Lives Matter movement, where we're going from here, what does justice look like, and what dismantling the police force means.

Quoted in Alyssa Vaughn, "Three Black Youth Activists on Organizing, Educating, and the Change They Hope to See," *Boston*, June 8, 2020. www.bostonmagazine.com.

population is relatively diverse, during their school years they were subjected to stereotyping. They also experienced microaggressions, which are brief, derogatory verbal or behavioral interactions that might not have been intended as such but were that nevertheless. They knew others who experienced similar interactions and more overt racism. After graduation they decided to survey fellow students about their experiences with race and communicate their findings in a letter to district administrators. In the letter, they pointed out issues such as lower graduation rates of Black and Hispanic students and a history curriculum that failed to include a robust telling of the Black experience. They also offered solutions such as a more diverse faculty, workshops for students and teachers on racism, and a more robust racially inclusive curriculum. The letter, which was shared on Twitter and other social media platforms, encouraged discussion within the district.

Some activists have found that no one tool achieves the level of communication they want. They have also found that sometimes the tools are less important than tailoring the message to one's audience. Jacory Martin, a Massachusetts high school junior in 2020, combines the reach of social media with the personal touch that comes through word of mouth. He believes that when communicating, whether on social media or in person, it is important to think about one's audience and how to motivate them. "We're organizing community events and vigils, we're promoting these movements on social media and by word of mouth, and we're asking ourselves things like, 'Who are we trying to target? Who are we trying to gather?'"[23]

In the weeks after George Floyd's death, Martin promoted activist events for youth. He persuaded them to come out and support racial justice by providing clear and direct information about the purpose and details of the events. He also used his skills to reach out to government leaders, including US representative Joe Kennedy of Massachusetts. When targeting government leaders, his goal is to get these leaders to support youths' actions for justice, and he does so by detailing the impacts of injustice on youths and why their support could make a difference.

> "We're organizing community events and vigils, we're promoting these movements on social media and by word of mouth, and we're asking ourselves things like, "Who are we trying to target? Who are we trying to gather?'"[23]
>
> —Jacory Martin, student activist

Time to Organize

Organization is essential for both small-scale and large-scale activist actions and events. Protests, in particular, require a great deal of planning and coordination. Protest planners need to set a date and time, choose a location and route (if the protest includes a march), and obtain needed permits from the city or town. Other organizational tasks include assigning speakers and providing technology, such as a sound system. In 2020 activist organizers also had to set up COVID-19 precautions by requiring and sometimes providing masks for protesters and including distancing between speakers.

A well-organized public protest can raise awareness, inspire action, and lead to change. Nupol Kiazolu, the president of Black Lives Matter of Greater New York and a student at Hampton University, has organized protests and seen their effects. She explains:

> Protesting and rallies are so important to the movement because it raises awareness on the issues that people would overlook if they didn't know about it or hear about it. I hear people often say, "Protesting doesn't work. Protesting doesn't matter." But I refute that all the way, because without that, you wouldn't know about the issues that are going on. I've been organizing for a really long time and protesting even longer. I've seen throughout my experience the impact that protesting actually has. It puts pressure on people in office, elected officials. It puts pressure on people in charge that are overseeing things.[24]

Young activists have also focused their efforts on organizing fund-raisers to further their cause. In Houston, Texas, in June 2020, Rice University students and alumni led a fund-raiser for local organizations that were working to eliminate race-based inequities in the criminal justice system. They set a goal of raising $2,500 in twenty-four hours. Instead, they raised $93,362. The keys to their success included communication and coordination. The fund-raiser was organized by Rice for Black Life (R4BL), a group made up of current and former Rice students. Members reached out to the university's department heads and senior administrators for support and donations. The university president gave the group access to lists of wealthy donors and other supporters, whom they also contacted.

Crowdsourcing is one of the new tools being embraced by activists. Crowdsourcing involves engaging a large group to support a common goal and typically is done through the internet, social media, and smartphone apps. In 2020 crowdsourcing was used as a tool for raising bail money for some of the people arrested at BLM protests. These efforts had raised tens of millions of dollars by June 2020. This was accomplished through social media and on crowdsourcing sites. The Minnesota Freedom Fund, a nonprofit organization that bails low-income people out of jail or immigration detention, usually runs on a tight budget. Its budget in 2018, for example, was about $150,000. In June 2020, however, it received $31 million from more than nine hundred thousand individual crowdsourced donations. Crowdsourcing has become a powerful tool in the activist arsenal.

All of this work helped the group exceed its fund-raising goal. "Our work today will help provide direct support to black folks, financially aid protestors . . . and promote . . . legislation to end debtors' prison, hold police accountable and reform the bail system,"[25] R4BL cofounder Summar McGee wrote at the conclusion of the event. R4BL's fund-raising success has resulted in queries for advice on how to achieve similar results from student-led organizations at over one hundred campuses.

Strong organizational skills can result in well-publicized, well-attended activist events, as students discovered at Haverford College in Pennsylvania. Three student groups led a fourteen-day strike and sit-in during October and November 2020. This event occurred in reaction to an email from college administrators requesting that students not protest the fatal shooting of Walter Wallace Jr., a Black man, by Philadelphia police on October 26, 2020. Administrators said they were concerned about student safety if a protest took place and spun out of control.

The email had the opposite effect, however. Angered by this request, students organized the strike and sit-in. They created a website, publicized their plans on social media, and drafted a letter urging the college president to more fully support racial and social justice on campus. Almost half of the college's more than

Asian protestors bring awareness at a sit-in in New York City. The COVID-19 pandemic, which originated in China, brought out a wave of hate crimes against Asian people, perpetrated by those blaming the pandemic on them. Being an activist requires substantial motivation and perseverance.

thirteen hundred students took part. The college responded by agreeing to budget for renovations to the Black Cultural Center and for antibias training for faculty and staff, strengthening recruitment and enrollment of Native American students, and hiring a new chief diversity officer. According to an email the leaders of these events sent out, "All the work we have done for this strike is more than just an attempt to make this institution safer for BIPOC [Black, Indigenous, people of color] students, we also hope to honor the lives taken from the system of white supremacist racial capitalism that Haverford itself continues to benefit from."[26] Due to the youth-led efforts, significant changes are taking place at Haverford.

Motivation

While education, communication, and organization are all necessary to become a successful activist, there is one more key component—motivation. Activism can be discouraging when the goals are not achieved. Change can be slow; it almost always requires time and effort. Activists have to learn how to maintain their motivation even when goals seem unachievable.

Sonia Harney, an activist with Roc 2 Change, a student-led organization in Rochester, New York, has found this to be true. Roc 2 Change conducts summits three times a year to get students and teachers from a cross section of schools to come together to discuss and understand race. They talk about problems that students of color deal with, such as being discouraged by counselors from taking Advanced Placement classes or hearing other students say that Black people cause crime. The summits also help students learn how to respond to these types of issues. They have discussed the difference between being nonracist and antiracist. A nonracist person might see or hear a racist encounter and not agree with what is taking place but also choose to say

> "For our generation, a big thing is getting rid of systemic racism. . . . This is the beginning of the war we're in for racial equality. And we can't lose hope."[27]
>
> —Sonia Harney, activist

nothing. An antiracist person, on the other hand, speaks out or intervenes when he or she encounters a racist event. Even alerting school authorities to such events is a form of taking action.

Harney focuses on getting students and teachers to be aware of and take action against racism in all its forms. "Every generation has its big issue to fight for," Harney says. "For our generation, a big thing is getting rid of systemic racism. . . . This is the beginning of the war we're in for racial equality. And we can't lose hope."[27]

CHAPTER FOUR

Risks and Rights

Travon Brown, a Black seventeen-year-old, decided to lead a racial justice protest in his mostly White hometown of Marion, Virginia. Brown says he had experienced racism in school and when applying for jobs. His own experiences, along with the horrible account of how George Floyd had died, inspired him to take a public stand. In June 2020 Brown led a march for justice from the Smyth County Courthouse to the local Walmart and then back to the courthouse. After reaching Walmart, the protesters knelt for eight minutes and forty-six seconds, which is how long the police officer held his knee on Floyd's neck. Brown emphasized that he wanted to demonstrate the power of peaceful protest.

And, in fact, Brown's protest was peaceful, but reaction to it was not. The night of the protest, Brown stayed at a friend's house. The next morning he received a text from his mother. She had come home from the store the night before to find a burning cross in the family's front yard. Police later arrested a next-door neighbor. Witnesses claimed he had admitted to the cross burning and had referred to the family using racial slurs. This action saddened and angered Brown, but he did not allow it to stop his fight for justice. Just three weeks after the incident, he led another protest. This time it attracted more than two hundred people. "When someone burnt that cross in my yard, that motivated me to go harder, that motivated me to go stronger for people of color, for African Americans,"[28] Brown explains.

As Brown discovered, activism sometimes comes with risks. The risks can be legal, as when arrests are made. The risks can be disciplinary, as when students are suspended or expelled. The risks can also lead to verbal abuse—in person or on social media—or, as in Brown's case, a threat of violence or actual violence.

Despite the risks, most activists are determined to continue their work. Being aware of the risks but also knowing one's rights are both essential elements of activism.

Harassment and Aggression

Public protests, even when done legally and peacefully, can still carry risks. Protesters in some of the BLM demonstrations have been subjected to ugly comments and physical aggression. Alicia Gee organized a BLM protest in the small town of Bethel, Ohio, on June 14, 2020. She expected about fifty people; the turnout was closer to one hundred. They were not alone, however. More than seven hundred counterprotesters also showed up. As cell phone videos show, the counterprotesters screamed racial slurs at the BLM protesters. They also became physically aggressive. "They were grabbing me, and grabbing my mom, and they just seemed to have no respect for the law,"[29] says Andrea Dennis, a Bethel resident who used Facebook Live to record and show a counterprotester grabbing a sign out of the hands of a BLM demonstrator. Another video from the protest shows a counterprotester punching a BLM protester in the back of the head. Incidents like this occurred at other protests throughout 2020.

According to the ACLU, counterprotesters have the right to attend a protest and voice their opposing views. However, they cannot physically stop the protest. And acts of physical aggression such as grabbing a sign from a person's hands or punching are

In 2020 counterprotesters in Mountain Village, Georgia, confront Black Lives Matter demonstrators. Many activists have been subjected to vulgar comments and physical aggression.

against the law. Depending on the circumstances, such actions could be considered assault.

A protester who encounters physical harassment from a counterprotester can try to defuse the situation by distancing themselves from the aggressors and/or can seek help from police. The police can arrest a person for assault or for disobeying police orders, such as being asked to disperse. Even if there has not been an assault, the police are allowed to separate opposing groups using barriers or other means if they deem it a safety issue. Ultimately, the ACLU explains, police officers are responsible for keeping members of the public safe during a demonstration and protecting the protesters' right to protest, no matter what they are protesting.

Excessive Force

Despite their role of protecting the public and maintaining order, in some instances police officers have been accused of using excessive force against protesters. Dounya Zayer experienced this while taking part in a BLM protest in New York City in May 2020. A video captured a male police officer forcefully shoving Zayer, then twenty, to the pavement at the protest. Zayer says she was not aggressive with the officer when he asked her to clear the area, but he shoved her anyway. The officer was later charged with misdemeanor assault and other offenses. He was also suspended without pay.

Activists who believe they have been subjected to excessive force by police have legal rights. The National Institute of Justice, the research arm of the US Department of Justice, explains that use of force by the police is only permitted under specific circumstances. These include a person resisting arrest, self-defense, or defense of others. Protesters who believe they have been subjected to unwarranted or excessive force can file a lawsuit in federal court. Such lawsuits usually revolve around claims of violations of constitutional rights, but these cases are not easily won. They require time and money—and a good lawyer. Additionally, a person has the right to video the police—and that video can be used as evidence in court. Cell phone videos have been used to prove that a person who was harmed or killed by police was not resisting arrest or threatening others.

Arrests

Arrest is another possible risk of activism. The right to protest is protected under the First Amendment to the Constitution. However, this does not give people the right to disobey laws. By mid-July 2020, more than ten thousand people had been arrested in BLM protests nationwide, according to an Associated Press tally. Los Angeles had the most arrests, followed by New York City, Dallas, and Philadelphia. The most common charges were curfew violations and failure to disperse. Some protesters were also charged with burglary and looting. While most of the arrests involved misdemeanors, or minor charges, activists should still understand that these arrests, if they result in convictions, can have long-term effects.

Nupol Kiazolu first became a racial justice activist at age twelve. That was the year Trayvon Martin, a Black teenager in Florida, was killed by George Zimmerman because Zimmerman assumed Martin was an intruder. On the phone with police, Zimmerman described Martin as wearing a hoodie. The hoodie became a symbol of assumptions made about Black people by others and law enforcement.

Kiazolu, a student in Georgia, read about the incident and people's accounts of it, thought about what happened, and decided her first step as an activist would be to wear a hoodie to school as a statement of solidarity with Martin. The problem was that hoodies were not allowed at her school. She was written up and sent to the principal's office for possible suspension. Her math teacher, who was supportive, went with her, and the principal told her to come back the next day with a case to support her decision. Kiazolu researched her First Amendment rights. She learned about a Supreme Court case, *Tinker v. Des Moines*, that ruled in favor of students who wore black armbands to protest the Vietnam War. Impressed with Kiazolu's argument and research, the principal allowed her to wear the hoodie. Kiazolu learned the value of educating oneself on rights and issues and went on to become a prominent activist who, as of 2021, was the president of Black Lives Matter of Greater New York.

D'Angelo Sandidge, a Black man in his twenties, had never protested before. But after he watched the video of George Floyd's death, he bought a poster board, wrote "no justice, no peace, no calmness in the street" on it, and went to a BLM protest in Indianapolis, Indiana. He ended up in jail, accused by police of violating curfew and resisting arrest. Police said that as he tried to run off, he put his hand in his backpack, where the police later found a Taser and a can of bear spray. Police claim he was going to use these items to resist arrest, but Sandidge says he keeps them there for protection. Sandidge, who has no criminal history or even an infraction on his driving record, could receive a year in prison and a fine of up to $5,000 if convicted of resisting arrest. If found guilty, this misdemeanor could remain on his record for life; it could come up in background checks, potentially making it more difficult to get a job. "I've never dealt with anything like this," says Sandidge. "I don't know what I'm going to do now."[30]

Although many people have taken part in protests without incident, the risk of arrest is real. It is important to understand that not following curfew, not leaving when police tell people to clear an area, and instigating any type of violence or looting can all be grounds for arrest. Even if one follows the laws, it is still possible to get caught up in an arrest, due to the chaos that can occur.

If stopped by police or arrested, people are still protected by the Constitution, explains the ACLU. Before an arrest takes place, people do not have to consent to any sort of search of their person or items, including electronics, but officers can frisk a person if they suspect a weapon. Even after an arrest, people have rights. Miranda rights entitle a person to remain silent and request an attorney. After an arrest, police can search the arrestee, including items like a backpack or phone. If police detain a minor, he or she can be questioned without having parents present. But if a minor is arrested, the minor has the right to request his or her parents' presence at any questioning. At any point during an interaction

A man protesting the killing of George Floyd is detained by police in Los Angeles in 2020. The right to protest is protected under the First Amendment, but it does not give people the right to disobey laws.

with police, if an activist feels his or her rights have been violated, the Legal Aid Society suggests the following: "When you can, write down everything you remember, including the officers' badge and patrol car numbers. Get contact information for witnesses. Take photographs of any injuries. Get medical treatment right away if you need it, and ask for a copy of any medical records."[31]

School Risks and Rights

Student activists are protected by the Constitution like everybody else in the United States. However, there are special risks for those who choose to take any action on school grounds. While students cannot be punished because they express their views on an issue, they can be punished if their speech or actions disrupt the school's functioning. Schools have a fair amount of discretion as to what is considered a disruption.

In a 1969 ruling, the Supreme Court affirmed the right of students to express themselves in school. This ruling came in the case of Mary Beth Tinker. Tinker was a thirteen-year-old junior high school student in December 1965 when she and a group of students decided to wear black armbands to school to protest the war in Vietnam. Tinker was suspended since the school had banned the armbands. The case was eventually heard by the Supreme Court, which ruled that students in school retain the right of freedom of expression. This freedom allows students to express their views through words, actions, or even clothes, but schools can punish students if their actions disrupt school activities.

In 2020 Kenton Vizdos was suspended after his silent protest during virtual school at Deep Run High School in Virginia because his actions were considered a disruption. Due to COVID-19, his school classes met virtually, where everyone could see one another via cameras on their computers. During class time, some teachers allowed students to turn off their cameras, and Vizdos used this time to play a slide show of images of Michael Brown, Breonna Taylor, and other victims of police violence. Teachers asked Vizdos to turn it off. He changed from a slide show to a

School walkouts can and do succeed in bringing about awareness and change. In February 2021 students at the all-girls Divine Savior Holy Angels High School in Milwaukee, Wisconsin, walked out of class. They were protesting what they viewed to be their school's failed policies on race. Prior to the walkout, a video posted on social media showed two White students at the school using a racial slur. Junior Laetitia Faye believes the video is evidence of a larger problem within the school. "These incidents have been going on for such a long time, and we're fed up," Faye said.

Prior to the walkout, school administrators released a statement saying that disciplinary steps had been taken against the students who had made the comments. But student protest organizers were not satisfied and wanted more change. The students said they wanted to see the school enact a zero-tolerance policy for racist incidents and more diversity education for students and staff. The administration chose to be supportive of the walkout, and no students were disciplined. Also, the administration has vowed to work with the students to commit to justice and equality in the school.

Quoted in Victor Jacobo, "Divine Savior Holy Angels Students Stage Walkout After Video Surfaces of White Students Using Racial Slur," CBS 58, February 25, 2021. www.cbs58.com.

static picture that listed the names of Black people killed by police. He was locked out of the virtual classes and subsequently suspended. Vizdos sought an appeal but was denied. He asked the ACLU to look at this case, and it represented him in a virtual hearing with the school's Student Support and Disciplinary Review Office. The ACLU believes the school suspended him because of the content of the images and not due to disruption. If true, this would mean that his rights were violated. "It appears to me that this case, particularly the static image, would be right in line with Tinker. It's not disrupting the class but it's still enabling the student to speak virtually,"[32] says JoAnn Koob, assistant law professor at George Mason University. The school decided to strike Vizdos's suspension from his record and allow him back in school. Since then, Vizdos has continued to use a picture of the names of Black people killed by police for his background picture during school.

Like Vizdos, two students in Florida wanted to show their support for BLM after an incident in their school. Since they attended a private school, they discovered they were more limited in what they could do. Jordana Codio and Khadee Hession, basketball players at American Heritage School in Florida, discovered the consequences of voicing their opinions on school grounds. They both decided to wear BLM shirts during a basketball warm-up before a game on December 4, 2020. They did this to protest a racial slur posted by another student in a virtual class. The two students wore the shirts again during three practices. And then they were told they could not wear the shirts again. Codio and Hession made it clear they still would wear them. The school canceled the next two games. Students believe the cancellations were due to the students' BLM shirts, since these go against the school's uniform policy. Eric Schwartzreich, an attorney for the school, responded that it was COVID-19 that resulted in the cancellations, but he also states, "By virtue of the fact that American Heritage is a private school they enjoy greater protection when it comes to regulation of student dress. Students at American Heritage all wear school uniforms. School uniforms minimize distractions and help maintain an orderly learning environment."[33]

Another form of school protest is walkouts, which students have organized as a way of protesting racism and other social and political issues. However, walkouts are not protected by the First Amendment, according to the ACLU. The ACLU explains that acts of civil disobedience that can be interpreted as interfering with the education of other students are not protected. A walkout is one such act. A school has the right to invoke discipline if the administration does not agree to allow a walkout. If students decide to hold a walkout, they can discuss their plan with the administration, but if the walkout is not approved, students need to understand that the school can punish them.

Escalation Risks

Another risk of activism is events potentially escalating to looting, vandalism, or violence. Although most attending protests,

People at a protest over the killing of George Floyd vandalize a police car in Los Angeles in 2020. Although most activists do not intend for riots and vandalizing to occur, high emotions and people with other agendas can cause lawlessness.

sit-ins, or marches do not intend for any type of violence or vandalism occurring, high emotions and people with other agendas can lead to lawlessness and violence. This occurred during some of the 2020 BLM protests. In Portland, Oregon, daily protests began on May 28, 2020, drawing thousands of protesters over a period of several months. The many peaceful protests were overshadowed by those that descended into riots, confrontations with police, and confrontations between the different groups of protesters. Looting, vandalism, and injuries occurred. At least one person was killed.

Other cities such as Seattle and Chicago also saw protests turn into riots. There were some who argued that rioting is a necessity to get people to pay attention to the issue, but most activists have said the violence is counterproductive. In Chicago, Jahmal Cole, founder and CEO of the social impact organization My Block, My Hood, My City, was frustrated by the looting in Chicago during the summer of 2020 and also upset that people confused peaceful protesters with these looters. He explains:

> I'm for protesting, I am not for senseless looting of communities that have been divested for so long. There's a right way to show resistance, constructive way to show resistance . . . I want to educate people that there's a difference between force and violence. Peaceful protesting is forceful, you can actually push policies and make a difference and get people to change by being forceful.[34]

Weighing the Risks

When taking action for a cause, activists should weigh all the risks, but they should also understand their rights. They should know that activism does lead to change, even if it does not always happen immediately. In 2020 former president Barack Obama gave a virtual commencement speech that was carried on network television and streamed to graduates of seventy-four historically Black colleges and universities across the United States. Obama spoke about the importance of grassroots activism as a way for the graduates to bring about racial justice. "Make sure you ground yourself in actual communities with real people—working whenever you can at the grassroots level. . . . Don't just activate yourself online. Change requires strategy, action, organizing, marching, and voting in the real world like never before."[35]

"Change requires strategy, action, organizing, marching, and voting in the real world like never before."[35]

—Barack Obama, former president of the United States

SOURCE NOTES

Introduction: Time to Act

1. Quoted in Jessica Bennett, "These Teen Girls Are Fighting for a More Just Future," *New York Times*, June 26, 2020. www.nytimes.com.
2. Quoted in Bennett, "These Teen Girls Are Fighting for a More Just Future."
3. Quoted in Bennett, "These Teen Girls Are Fighting for a More Just Future."
4. Quoted in Kimberly Aleah, "Youth Organizers: Brianna Chandler & Khalea Edwards of Sunrise STL and Occupy City Hall STL," Yahoo! Money, October 8, 2020. https://money.yahoo.com.

Chapter One: The Issue Is Racial Justice

5. Quoted in Leonard Greene, "'This is About Equal Justice': Petition Urges Manhattan DA to Prosecute Tourist Over Racial Phone Flap," *New York Daily News*, January 4, 2021. www.nydailynews.com.
6. Elie Mystal, "Breonna Taylor Was Murdered for Sleeping While Black," *The Nation*, May 15, 2020. www.thenation.com.
7. American Civil Liberties Union, "Racial Profiling: Definition," 2021. www.aclu.org.
8. Ivy Morgan, "Students of Color Face Steep School Funding Gaps," Education Trust, February 26, 2018. https://edtrust.org.
9. Quoted in Sheryl Nance-Nash, "Racial Bias in Mortgage Lending Is Very Real, but There Are Steps You Can Take to Secure a Loan When the Odds Are Stacked Against You," *Business Insider*, June 9, 2020. www.businessinsider.com.
10. Quoted in PressFrom, "Kept Out: How Banks Block People of Color from Homeownership," February 15, 2018. https://pressfrom.info.
11. Quoted in Gina Chung, "Free Speech 2020: An Interview with Nupol Kiazolu," PEN America, August 6, 2020. https://pen.org.

Chapter Two: The Activists

12. Quoted in Madison Feller, "These Teen Black Lives Matter Activists Are Writing the Future," *Elle*, July 20, 2020. www.elle.com.

13. Quoted in Tiffany Silva, "Sixteen-Year-Old Thandiwe Abdullah Is Making a Difference Championing for Black Lives Matter," BCK, June 4, 2020. https://bckonline.com.
14. Quoted in Color of Change, "The Loudest Voice: Corporate America Needs to Get on the Right Side of History. Civil Rights Nonprofit Color of Change Gets It There—Ready or Not," 2021. https://colorofchange.org.
15. Quoted in Color of Change, "Civil Rights Group Demands That FOX Drop *Cops* After 25 Years of Exploiting Negative Racial Stereotypes," 2021. https://colorofchange.org.
16. Quoted in National Association for the Advancement of Colored People, "NAACP Applauds Supreme Court Victory in *NAACP v. Trump*," June 20, 2020. www.naacp.org.
17. Quoted in Ava Dunwoody, "Students Prepare to Volunteer on Election Day," *Baylor Lariat*, October 28, 2020. https://baylorlariat.com.
18. Quoted in Kimberly Aleah, "Youth Organizers: Madison Crenshaw, Buckhead for Black Lives," Yahoo!, October 12, 2020. www.yahoo.com.
19. Quoted in Sarah Holcomb, "The Teenagers Pushing for Radical Change in Portland's Police System," Next City, June 11, 2020. https://nextcity.org.

Chapter Three: The Teen Activist's Tool Kit

20. Quoted in Seth Kaplan, "'I Was like a Volcano'—York Teens Who Organized Summer Protest Reflect on Aftermath of George Floyd's Death," ABC27 News, February 10, 2021. www.abc27.com.
21. Quoted in Alyssa Vaughn, "Three Black Youth Activists on Organizing, Educating, and the Change They Hope to See," *Boston*, June 8, 2020. www.bostonmagazine.com.
22. Quoted in Elle McLogan, "Social Media's Role in the Racial Justice Movement: 'The Conversation Is Moving So Much More Quickly,'" CBS New York, July 10, 2020. https://newyork.cbslocal.com.
23. Quoted in Vaughn, "Three Black Youth Activists on Organizing, Educating, and the Change They Hope to See."
24. Quoted in Chung, "Free Speech 2020."
25. Quoted in Greta Anderson, "Organizing for Change," Inside Higher Ed, June 6, 2020. www.insidehighered.com.
26. Quoted in Rebecca Raber, "Student Protest Brings Racial Equity Advances," Haverford College, November 13, 2020. www.haverford.edu.
27. Quoted in Justin Murphy and Adria R. Walker, "Teens from Rochester to Hilton Feel Outraged So They're Rallying Against Injustice," *Rochester (NY) Democrat & Chronicle*, October 19, 2020. www.democratandchronicle.com.

Chapter Four: Risks and Rights

28. Quoted in Tim Dodson, "Watch Now: Cross Burning Victim Led Marion's Black Lives Matter March," *Bristol (VA) Herald Courier*, July 4, 2020. https://heraldcourier.com.

29. Quoted in Adrian Horton, "Hundreds of Armed Counter-Protesters Confront Black Lives Matter Rally in Ohio," *The Guardian* (Manchester, UK), June 18, 2020. www.theguardian.com.

30. Quoted in Melissa Chan, "These Black Lives Matter Protesters Had No Idea How One Arrest Could Alter Their Lives," *Time*, August 19, 2020. https://time.com.

31. Legal Aid Society, "What You Need to Know About Your Rights as a Protester," October 27, 2020. https://legalaidnyc.org.

32. Quoted in Arianna Coghill, "Do Students Have a Right to Protest? Henrico Case Raises Questions," Dogwood, December 3, 2020. https://vadogwood.com.

33. Quoted in Austen Erblatt and Adam Lichtenstein, "How Two Students' Black Lives Matter Display Has Stirred Emotions at This Private School," *Fort Lauderdale (FL) Sun Sentinel*, December 15, 2020. www.sun-sentinel.com.

34. Quoted in Erica Gunderson, "Riot or Rebellion: Why Peaceful Protests Can Become Violent," WTTW, June 1, 2020. https://news.wttw.com.

35. Quoted in Anne Dennon, "Students Demand Racial Justice and Equity on Campus," Best Colleges, June 17, 2020. www.bestcolleges.com.

WHERE TO GO FOR
IDEAS AND INSPIRATION

Books

Robin DiAngelo, *White Fragility*. Boston: Beacon, 2018.

Stuart A. Kallen, *Teen Guide to Student Activism*. San Diego, CA: ReferencePoint, 2019.

Ibram X. Kendi, *How to Be an Antiracist*. London: One World, 2019.

Beverly Tatum, *Why Are All the Black Kids Sitting Together in the Cafeteria? And Other Conversations About Race*. New York: Basic Books, 2017.

Organizations and Other Websites

American Civil Liberties Union (ACLU)
www.aclu.org

The ACLU organization defends people's constitutional rights. The organization's website provides information about racial justice, student rights, and current legal activities for justice. The website provides specific cases the ACLU is working on and their status. It also provides a section that allows people to find out how they can take action.

Black Lives Matter (BLM)
https://blacklivesmatter.com

The Black Lives Matter Global Network Foundation is a global organization with the overall goal to rid the world of White supremacy and help organize actions in Black communities to fight for this goal. The BLM website has specific goals of the organization and tool kits for activists. It also provides social media graphics for activists to show support on their social media.

National Association for the Advancement of Colored People (NAACP)
www.naacp.org

Established in 1909, the NAACP is a civil rights organization in the United States that works to advance justice. Its website provides information on its latest actions and how people can become involved. The website also provides recommendations for policies that government should implement.

Racial Justice for Youth: A Toolkit for Defenders
https://defendracialjustice.org

The website for Racial Justice for Youth: A Toolkit for Defenders provides youth activists the training, resources, and information needed to work toward racial justice. It discusses how to fight over-policing, over-criminalization, and school exclusion of students of color.

News Articles

BBC, "Breonna Taylor: Timeline of Black Deaths Caused by Police," BBC, January 6, 2021. www.bbc.com.

Roby Chatterji, "Fighting Systemic Racism in K–12 Education: Helping Allies Move from the Keyboard to the School Board," Center for American Progress, July 8, 2020. www.americanprogress.org.

Precious Fondren, "Young Black Activists Are Leading the Movement for Black Lives," *Teen Vogue*, July 9, 2020. www.teenvogue.com.

History, "Black History Milestones: Timeline," February 10, 2021. www.history.com.

Meera Jagannathan, "'Black History Is American History': How to Educate Yourself and Work Toward Racial Equity This Month (and Beyond)," MarketWatch, February 12, 2021. www.marketwatch.com.

Atticus LeBlanc, "How Systemic Racism Exists in U.S. Housing Policies," *Forbes*, July 9, 2020. www.forbes.com.

Opportunity Agenda, "Ten Lessons for Talking About Race, Racism, and Racial Justice," 2020. www.opportunityagenda.org.

Documentaries

Ken Burns, Sarah Burns, and David McMahon, dirs., *Central Park Five*. Arlington, VA: PBS, 2012.

Ava Duvernay, dir., *13th*. Forward Movement, Oakland, CA: Kandoo Films, and Netflix, 2016.

Jennifer Furst, dir., *TIME: The Kalief Browder Story*. New York: Cinemart/ The Weinstein Company, 2017.

Laurens Grant, dir., *Stay Woke: The Black Lives Matter Movement*. Santa Monica, CA: United States: FarWord, 2016.

Nadia Hallgren, dir., *Becoming*. New York: Big Mouth Productions and Higher Ground Productions, 2020.

David Lindsay and T.J. Martin, dirs., *LA92*. Los Angeles, CA: National Geographic and Lightbox, 2017.

INDEX

PICTURE CREDITS

ABOUT THE AUTHOR

Leanne K. Currie-McGhee lives in Norfolk, Virginia, with her husband, Keith, two daughters, Grace and Hope, and dog, Delilah. She has written educational books for two decades.